The Darkest Pen

By James Lefay
Bishop

Dedication:

This book is dedicated to Rose. The best grandma anyone could ask for.

And to my lovely wife, Vivian Vandam. You keep me inspired, even on my worst days. I love you so much!

This is a collection of poems composed by various vampires, ranging from the famous, to the forgotten. Please, grab your wine and sit; share this experience with me.

The names on the bottom of these poems are from The Ascent from Chaos Trilogy.

James Lefay Bishop.

The River.

While staring into the darkness

I see a small light.

What can this be, I ask.

I traverse the emptiness.

The light leads to a crimson river.

I'm horrified...but fascinated.

A small raft sits before me, and it
makes me shiver.

Do I dare follow it?

Compelled, I get in with trembling
knees.

The raft moves and I watch

Painful images of my past reflect from
the crimson.

Tears of shame run down my face, for I tried so hard to please.

Ashamed, I close my eyes and bury my face.

Voice of those I've wronged surround me.

"I'm sorry!" I cry, "Please forgive me! I was wrong!"

Then, there was silence.

I open my eyes and see I'm docked.

I turn to the water and it's normal.

I draw in a breath and turn back around,

Shocked to be back home.

Some say that life is like a tapestry.

I say it flows more like a river

And sometimes, you have to look

Into the Reflections to see who you
truly are.

Penned by James Lefay.

Pain

Mortals cry about their pain…

They have no right.

It was their kind who waged war.

We suffered the consequences.

My father fought to preserve our race.

He fought, in part, to save the mortals too.

They were blinded by The Slayers.

So to were we, to one of our own.

Atop the watch tower, the traitor signaled,

And they ambushed us.

My Father fought valiantly

But he was overwhelmed.

Despite the traitor we won.

But the cost was too great.

My father was gone.

The only thing left was his gold dagger.

I wear it with pride

But even now, I lack his wisdom.

Before *they* came, I sulked, and
wallowed in self-pity.

Like mortals before me, I had all but
given up.

My father would have been ashamed.

I could hear his disappointment.

But I was shown a better way,

And now we thrive!

But I will never forget

The Anguish of losing my father,

My Maker. Long Live the King.

Long Live, Castle Carlcinni.

Penned by King Vincenzo Carlcinni,
son of the late King.

The Woods/Bidden

We are the lost.

We are the forgotten.

We paid the greatest cost.

We survive,

Deep within the Bidden.

In darkness, we thrive.

Our Humanity is no more.

Our tongues are shriveled.

Our eyes…our eyes are so sore.

Hunger is all we feel,

Hunger is all we know.

With this Hunger, our fate will seal.

Penned by a nameless vampire, who succumbed to the hunger of fellow ferals.

Madness

Sitting in his corner,

He rocks back and forth.

Waiting.

His blood shot eyes

Scan the darkness.

He laughs at the shadows.

"Emilio," he giggles. "I'm going to get
you!"

Jealousy and Rage...

These are constants.

But deep down

He feels shame.

And loneliness.

Force Turned by his maker,
Violated, and abandoned,
He hones his hate on his rival.

He didn't want a rival.
He wanted a friend.
But his pride and ego refused.

He sits in wait.
Rocking back and forth.
He is...Marcas.

Penned by a younger, sane Marcas.
Rival of James Lefay.

Never Alone

No one ever truly

Leaves this place.

The world is vile, and cruelly

Uses its wicked hand to slap my face.

When I'm anguishing,

I run to the fog, for they're there.

They cure me of life's ravishing.

They embrace me and smooth my hair.

I go there when I feel scared.

I go there when I need to see, to hear.

No one will follow me, no one has
dared.

For in the Fog, I can lose my fear.

I see them all.

I feel the light they shone.

I will never fall.

In the Fog, I am Never Alone.

Penned by an unknown vampire.

Confinement

Confined to a dungeon,

My hunger roars in my ears.

It shakes me from the

Inside out.

My own devilish desires

Placed me here, but

I can't believe my love

Would abandon me.

He used to send me

The broken, The maimed.

Even the very ill.

But soon, only corpses were bestowed.

Like my maker before me,
I feasted on the fallen.
Servants and vampires alike.
Vile, and taboo, it made me strong.

Venomous hate drips from my fangs
As I think about my former beloved...
But he is dead...and my rage and venom
Are unfocused.

I've turned another to stop me
From making similar mistakes
But his hunger matches my own...
We must leave this place.

We are hunters,
Locked in a rotten, gilded cage.

We are slaves to our hunger,

But they won't let us go.

Do I help my captors?

Or do I stew in Venom?

My fledgling awaits my bidding.

What will come of us?

Penned by Adria. Former Queen and prisoner of King Adrian Carlcinni. Is she free? Or is she indeed trapped?

The Flame

For years I searched
To find my parent's killers.
But they've always lurched
Away from me.

I train, and train,
But I know deep down
In my heart, and in my brain,
That I will always frown...

They're masters of killing.
Masters of hiding.
But even more chilling,
They hide in plain sight.

I feel them taunting me

And it fills me with rage.

I try so hard to see,

But it's impossible to turn the page.

I'm one of them now,

But even so

I fear they'll make me bow

At their disgusting feet and face their
wretched show.

But my love is with me,

And he will help me slay.

For the Twins can't see

That we've changed the game they play.

Penned by Jillian Rose Edwards,
Former Slayer, and fledgling of Sevrin.

View of the World

Ancient blood runs through my veins.

I live, but I will never die.

I've watched mankind rise,

And I will watch them fall.

Mankind only understands destruction,

And for that I pity them.

I've seen death more times

Then any mortal could understand.

Destruction is not a means to an end.

It is a means to enact more death.

Mankind is lost...

I've tried to help them...

But I can't force them to heed wisdom.

I can't force them to value their lives.

I can't force them into acceptance...

They have defeated me.

Penned by Dauntus, The First
Vampire.

Growth

A Millennium has passed
And despite their growth,
Mankind is still so young.

They are Naïve,
And filled with angst,
But they are not totally lost.

I believe they can be taught.
They can learn.
But we must put aside our pity.

Control and power are different.
Having power, means just that.
Having control, means you have the
wisdom to use power.

Once they realize that,
They will be better for it.
I've seen sparks of brilliance.

Even acceptance.
But the fault is not solely theirs.
We must do our part.

We must use our
Age and our power
To educate them.

We can help them.
We can help all of them.
We need each other.

Penned by Athen Sevrinus, or Sevrin,
as he is known as by his
contemporaries.

The Beast

I gave you your first breath

For your first cry

And I'll be there to take it

When you die.

What am I?

I am the rage that dwells

Deep inside.

I am the Anguish that brings

You to your knees.

What am I?

I can give you the power

To topple mountains.

I can take that power

And rob you of your dreams.
What am I?

I am the darkness
That clouds men's thoughts
I am the Monster that dwells
In Men's hearts.
What am I?

I
Am
The Beast.

Penned by The Beast.

Upcoming projects!

As of now, the fourth book in the Ascent from Chaos series is still being written.

Additionally, a re write of my very first book is in the works as well. Prodigy. Prodigy is the story of one James Lefay, a vampire prodigy who gets into more than his fair share of battles and even embarrassing situations.

I am also working on a fantasy novel as well. This is still in the early stages, but I do plan to finish it.

Thank you all so much for taking the time to read this, or any of my other works. It means so much to me! If anyone has any questions, please contact me at vampireauthor@comcast.net.

I appreciate all the support and look forward to meeting everyone at future book signings!

www.ingramcontent.com/pod-product-compliance
Lightning Source LLC
Chambersburg PA
CBHW020137180726
47992CB00023B/3233